To all teachers and all educators who willingly and patiently teach our children. Pipsie, Alfred, and I are dedicated to opening young minds to the world of nature. You open curious minds to everything they will need to chase their dreams.
—R.D.

For Andrew— keep on exploring!
—T.B.

Acknowledgments
Thank you to all the wonderful people who allowed me to read Pipsie: Megan, Gary, Kim W., Alice, Kim L., Dot, Patti and Sasha, Frann, Tim, Marina, Roy and Donna, Carol, Debbie, and many thanks to the Delaware Children's Museum, The Young Bean, and the Hagley Museum.
—R.D.

A LURIE INK Book

Text copyright © 2017 by Rick DeDonato
Illustrations copyright © 2017 by Tracy Bishop

Published by Two Lions, New York
www.apub.com

Amazon, the Amazon logo, and Two Lions are trademarks of Amazon.com, Inc., or its affiliates.

ISBN-13: 9781503950993
ISBN-10: 1503950999

Book design by Tanya Ross-Hughes

Printed in China

First Edition

10 9 8 7 6 5 4 3 2 1

PIPSIE
nature detective
TURTLE TROUBLE

Written by Rick DeDonato
Illustrated by Tracy Bishop

two lions

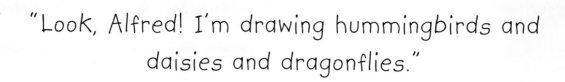

"Look, Alfred! I'm drawing hummingbirds and daisies and dragonflies."

Pipsie and Alfred Z. Turtle sat in Pipsie's tree house drawing all the things they saw in the park that morning.

I'm drawing a picture of my peanut butter and jelly sandwich.

Then Pipsie noticed Alfred was doing something he never did. "Alfred, why are you drawing with your LEFT FOOT?" Pipsie asked. "You're RIGHT-FOOTED!"

Alfred showed her his right foot. It was
grassy and had a BIG bump.

Pipsie touched his foot. "It's sticky!" she cried.

And it hurts too.

"Alfred, something bit you!
Let's go back to the park to
find out what it was.

"But first you need to take a bath! You have a terrible case of the SMELLIES. Maybe that has something to do with your bite."

Baths... YUCK!

At the park, Pipsie and Alfred began to look for clues to their BUMPY, STICKY, STINKY mystery. After all, Pipsie was a nature detective.

"Wow! An ant parade!" Pipsie said. "And they're all carrying food. Did you know an ant's most important job is to feed everybody in the nest?"

My most important job is to feed me.

"Hmmm. There's nothing sticky here, Alfred," said Pipsie. "And nothing stinky. So I don't think an ant bit your foot. Let's keep looking."

"Mosquitoes BUZZ . . . and they BITE! Maybe a mosquito bit you."

Pipsie knew where there were lots of mosquitoes: down at the lake. So that's where she and Alfred went next.

"Mosquitoes need water to hatch their eggs," said Pipsie.
"This is a BIG lake—and that means there are
a gazillion eggs here!"

And a GAZILLION mosquitoes!

"But there's nothing sticky or stinky here," said Pipsie. "And mosquito bites are itchy. So I don't think a mosquito bit you."

Then Pipsie shouted, "Alfred! A snake! Let's go look!"

A snake? Let's go home!

"Isn't this fun?" Pipsie said, bouncing on the snake.

But Alfred was already on his way.
"Don't worry! This snake doesn't bite!"

Pipsie noticed that Alfred
was staring up at the trees.
"Looks like you found a clue!"
She ran over to him.

Above them, a yellow-and-black spider
dangled from her beautiful web.

I stopped to say
HELLO to this spider
this morning.

"Hmmm," said Pipsie. "Spiderwebs ARE sticky. But this web is WAY UP THERE. And you're WAY DOWN HERE. No way that web made your foot sticky. And there's nothing stinky around here."

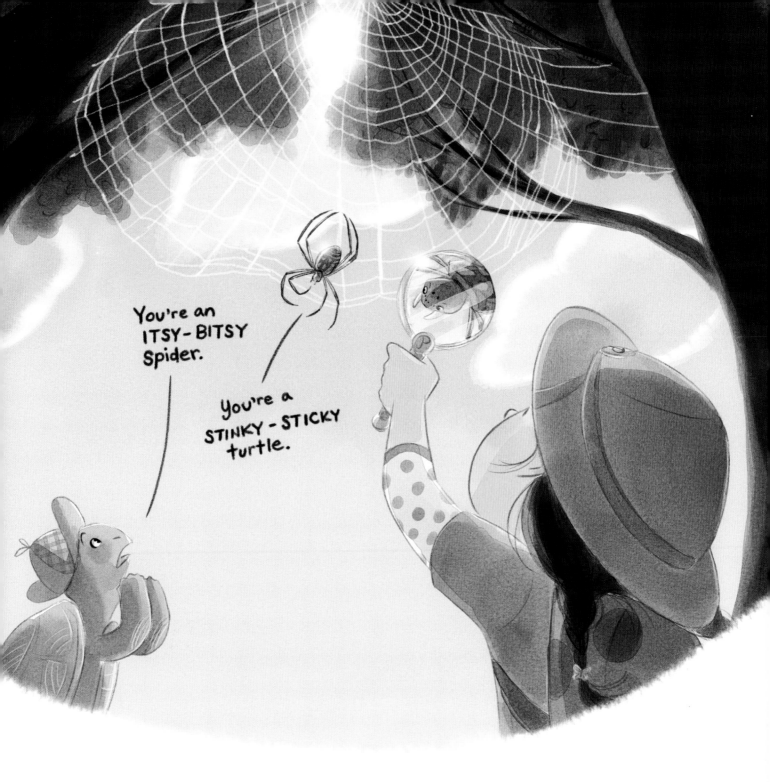

Pipsie looked at the spider with her magnifying glass. "Alfred, I don't think this spider bit you. She's a garden spider. Garden spiders don't usually bite."

"This is one TRICKY mystery." Pipsie scratched her head.

Suddenly, a STINKY SMELL blew their way.

"Alfred, do you smell what I smell?" Pipsie asked. "P-U-U-U-U . . . This could be just the stinky clue we need! LET'S MAKE THIS MYSTERY HISTORY!"

Pipsie and Alfred followed the smell to the apple tree . . .

This smells like trouble to me.

. . . where they found some little flat bugs.

Alfred showed Pipsie how he gave the bugs a ride that morning by sending the apple rolling down the hill!

"These are STINKBUGS," said Pipsie. "When you touch them, they let out a stink to protect themselves. The bad smell keeps everyone away."

I think I might need LESS STINKY friends.

"Oh, Alfred, you just touched the stinkbug. I think you might need ANOTHER bath!" Pipsie cried.

"Now we know what made you stink," Pipsie said. "But these stinkbugs didn't bite you, and they aren't sticky. So we haven't solved the whole mystery yet." She took out her notebook and read her list of clues.

	STICKY	STINKY	BUZZY
ANTS	NO	NO	NO
MOSQUITOES	NO	NO	YES
SPIDERWEB	YES	NO	NO
STINKBUGS	NO	YES	NO

"Alfred, what did you do after the bugs rolled down the hill?" Pipsie asked. But Alfred didn't answer.

He was chasing the apple
just like he did that morning.
He ran after it s—l—o—w—l—y
because that's how turtles run.

He followed it down the hill . . .

. . . around the tree . . .

. . . and right into
the flower garden!

The apple bumped into the daisies.
Daisy pollen flew up in the air—
and Alfred sneezed!

A-C-H-O-O!
Yep. Just like this morning.

Then Alfred sneezed again.
So loudly that it knocked Pipsie's notebook out of her hand.
And so loudly that it woke up something above them . . .

. . . something BUZZY!

"Honeybees . . . and a hive!"
Pipsie cried. "Alfred, bees are
dangerous! I think a bee stung you!
MYSTERY SOLVED!"

When I see a BEE,
I need to BEE careful!

"But wait. . . . That hive is too high for
you to reach. So how did you get STICKY?
Mystery NOT solved."

Pipsie picked up her notebook. It was STICKY.

"Look, it's honey from the hive. Your foot must have gotten sticky when you stepped in it."

Pipsie spotted something. "Quick, Alfred, run!"

When they were far enough away, Pipsie pointed to the grass under the hive. "Look, Alfred! Those are wasps! Wasps love honey, and they buzzzzz and sting, too! You got stung by a WASP!"

"This BUMPY, STINKY, STICKY, BUZZY, TRICKY MYSTERY is finally HISTORY!"

Turtle Trouble solved! Now let's buzzzzz outta here!

FUN FACTS

BEES are important *because they* POLLINATE lots and lots of flowers. As a bee flies from flower to flower, the pollen from the part of the flower called the anther sticks to its wings. Then the pollen falls from the *bee's* wings onto the part of the flower called the pistil. Next, the pollen moves down the pistil to the eggs, and *seeds are made!* Flowers and fruits and vegetables grow from the seeds. So the next time *you're* eating a fruit or veggie, you can thank a *bee!*

The average honeybee will produce 1/12 of a teaspoon of honey in its lifetime.

ANTS are VERY strong. They can carry 50 times their own body weight. If people had the same strength as ants, we could lift a small car above our heads.

Why don't **SPIDERS** stick to their own webs? Because only the inside part of the web is made of sticky silk. The outside edges and the straight spokes of the web are really strong and NOT STICKY, and that is where the spider walks. The spider has to learn this path or it WILL get caught in its own web!

STINKBUGS are stinky because they have stink glands between their first and second pairs of legs. If a stinkbug feels threatened, or is injured or moved, it lets out an odor to protect itself—just like a skunk does!

Only female **MOSQUITOES** will "bite" you. Male mosquitoes don't feed on humans; they eat only plant nectar.
Mosquitoes feed mostly at night and will fly up to 14 miles looking for someone to feed on.

Insect Insight by John Moore, MS Entomology

Stink Bug

Pipsie's Nature Notebook